THIS CANDLEWICK BOOK BELONGS TO:

Second U.S. edition 1996

Library of Congress Catalog Card Number 95-67159

ISBN 1-56402-574-8

2 4 6 8 10 9 7 5 3 1

Printed in Hong Kong

The pictures in this book were done in watercolor and ink.

Candlewick Press
2067 Massachusetts Avenue
Cambridge, Massachusetts 02140

# TELL US ~A~ STORY

*Allan Ahlberg*

illustrated by

*Colin McNaughton*

CANDLEWICK PRESS

CAMBRIDGE, MASSACHUSETTS

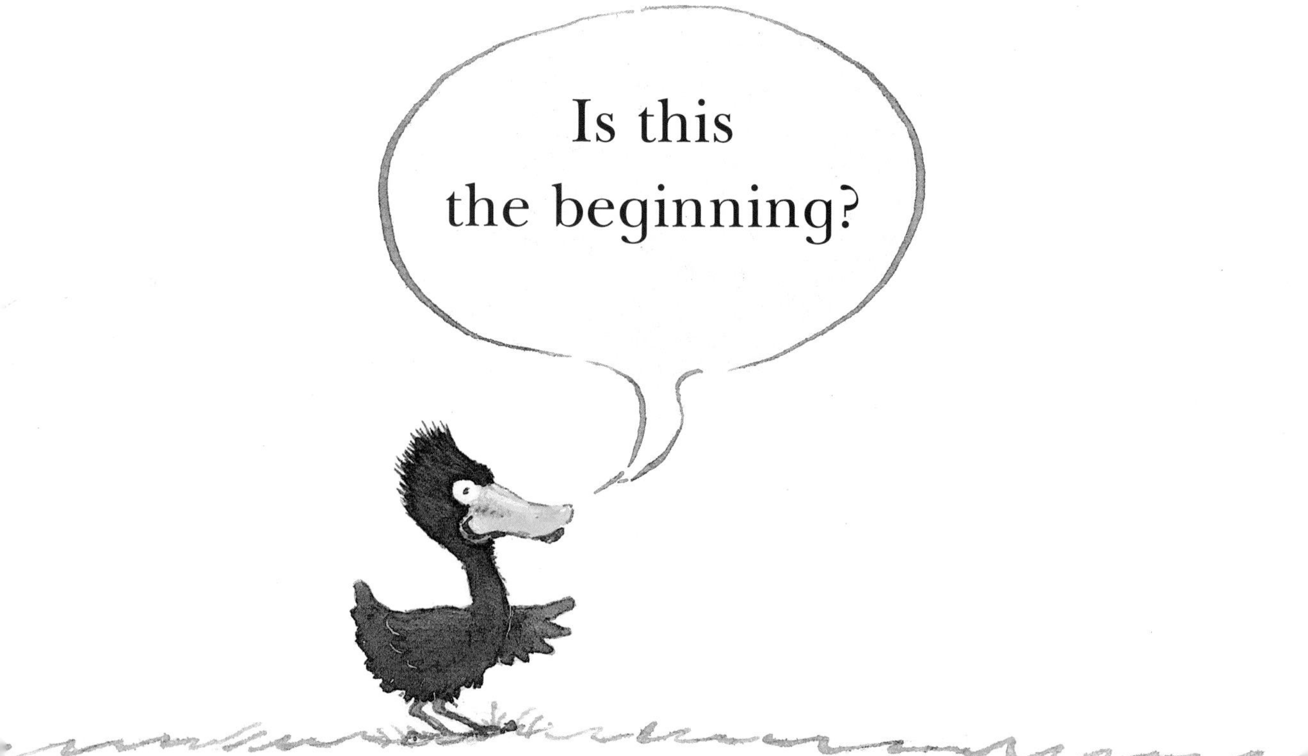
Is this
the beginning?

# Contents

# The Pig

Two little boys
climbed up to bed.

"Tell us a story, Dad,"
they said.

"Okay!" said Dad.
"There was once a pig
who ate too much
and got so big
he couldn't sit down,
he couldn't bend. . . .

So he ate standing up
and got bigger—The End!"

The End!

# The Cat

"That story's no good, Dad,"
the little boys said.
"Tell us a better one instead."

"Okay!" said Dad.
"There was once a cat
who ate too much
and got so fat

he split his fur,
which he had to mend
with a sewing machine
and a zipper—The End!"

# The Horse

"That story's too crazy, Dad,"
the little boys said.

"Tell us another one instead."

"Okay!" said Dad.
"There was once a horse
who ate too much
and died, of course—

The End."

# The Cow

"That story's too sad, Dad,"
the little boys said.
"Tell us a happier one instead."

"Okay . . . " said Dad.
"There was once a cow
who ate so much
that even now

she fills two fields

and blocks a road,

and when they milk her
she has to be towed!

She wins gold cups
and medals too,
for the creamiest milk
and the *loudest* moo!"

Moo!

"Now that's the end,"
said Dad. "No more."
And he shut his eyes
and began to snore.

Then the two little boys
climbed out of bed
and crept downstairs . . .

to their mom instead.

# The End

ALLAN AHLBERG was born in 1938. He worked as a postman and a plumber before becoming an elementary school teacher and, eventually, a principal. He currently coauthors books with his wife, illustrator Janet Ahlberg. Their books include *The Jolly Postman*.

COLIN McNAUGHTON has been drawing monsters and dinosaurs, giants and pirates since he was a boy. His sense of humor remains as childlike as ever, which perhaps explains why he is so popular with young readers. He has published more than fifty titles in the United States and England, including *Making Friends with Frankenstein, Jolly Roger,* and *Captain Abdul's Pirate School.*